WHAT ABOUT JOHNSON?

What We Don't Know Can Hurt Us

Harvell Johnson

Word on da Street Publishing
Norcross, GA 30093

What About Johnson?

ISBN 978-0-9885056-0-5

Genre: Realistic Fiction

Publisher: Word on da Street Publishing

Email: llperry803@gmail.com

Website: www.wordondastreetpublishing.org

Book Cover Design: Donna Osborn Clark at CreationByDonna.com

Editor: Vanetta Howard
vanettahoward@yahoo.com

Typeset & Interior Design: www.CreationByDonna.com

Word on Da Street Publishing
Norcross, GA 30093

This book is dedicated to my kids, Kyle, Sunset and Harvell. It is also dedicated to all of the children who feel as though they are wearing a mask and people not being able to relate to them.

Acknowledgments

I want to thank Jesus, my publisher, Word on da Street Publishing, Mrs. Donna Osborn Clark, my wife Makeda, and all of those who have supported me in making this book possible

I would also like to thank Kenneth R. Woolley III, at the Allentown Public Library for helping me when I needed it the most and for his complete undivided attention.

Introduction

This is a story about a nine year old boy named Johnson who lives in Brooklyn, New York with his mother who would later find out what it's like living as if he were wearing a mask, and people not knowing what was on his mind. The mask is not physical but mental, which later in life turns into reality. After practicing a positive lifestyle, he communicates better and finds himself. After certain life matters, Johnson converts into a bright intelligent young man that's very helpful in many ways to others, including himself.

WHAT ABOUT JOHNSON?
What We Don't Know Can Hurt Us

Harvell Johnson

CHAPTER ONE

Today was a good day in school. I wonder what mommy is making for dinner. I hope it's my favorite; hot dogs, rice and beans and a nice big cup of Kool Aid!

"Mom can you help me with my home work?" I asked.

"Yes, give me a minute, baby."

Man, I wonder why my mother sometimes comes out of the bathroom confused or tired but then snaps back to normal. No matter what, she is my mom. As I got started on my homework, I smelled the aroma and couldn't wait until I was done so I could go outside to play.

Three times three equals nine. Twelve plus two hundred eighteen equals two hundred thirty.

"Baby, come eat and I'll finish up your homework with you!" mom yelled.

"Ok mom, I'm coming!"

After dinner, I headed back to my room to finish up my homework. Mom came in and sat on my bed. "Your room looks clean," she said, looking around.

I was hoping mom would give me a dollar or two to get some junk food. I knew she never had much money. But being the only child, I always had what I needed and sometimes more.

"Ok baby, you're getting better in all your subjects, keep up the good work!" Mom smiled.

My mother knew math was my worst subject and that I needed to improve or I would have to go to summer school so I wouldn't get held back.

"All done mom!"

"Ok." she replied.

"Can I go outside to play now?"

"Of course, just make sure you're in before it gets dark and don't make me come out there looking for you!" Mom warned.

I jumped on my skate board and rode about a half block away to the store with the money my mom gave me. I bought ten packs of Now and Laters, cookies, and a big bag of chips. I would always buy candy to take to school the next day even though I knew I wasn't supposed to eat it in class. Sometimes I would put a pack of Now and Laters on the radiator in the back of the class so they would melt and then eat them. I opened a pack of cherry and chomped down on them. I hopped on my skateboard and rode past a girl I like named Lisa. Lisa goes to my school but is in a grade higher than me.

"Hello Johnson," said Lisa.

"Hello Lisa, where are you going?"

"Nowhere, just riding around trying to learn some new tricks."

I think she knew I liked her but never showed it. But if what my mother says about girls always knowing if a boy likes them or not is true, then I guess she knows. As we get near the Brooklyn museum we sat down and watched the other kids play at the Johnny pump.

"That looks like fun," I said to Lisa.

"Yeah, you want to go in and get wet?" she asked.

"Nah, I'm going to sit here for a while and relax."

I was never a sociable person. I was always alone or with the same few friends most of the time. Sometimes I would go to Manhattan with my cousin Junior to ride the

Staten Island ferry without my mother's permission. I was kind of young to be riding trains alone, but living in one of the worst parts of Brooklyn, I grew up fast and learned quick. After playing for a few hours, I decided to go home to check on my mother. Although mom was much older than I was and could take care of herself, as the only child I felt like we had to take care of each other because we were all each other had.

I came home at about six thirty. It was about to get dark outside and I wanted to relax and snack on something. As I opened the door, my mother was coming out of the bathroom. I went to the bathroom to wash my hands and saw what looked like a needle on the floor. I recognized what it was because I have asthma and have been rushed numerous times to the emergency room to get asthma shots. I always heard about drugs and people that used them. *But not my mom.*

I picked up the needle and threw it in the trash can. After coming out of the bathroom, I made myself a peanut butter and jelly sandwich, ate oatmeal cookies, and chugged down some orange juice. My mother asked me how my day was. I told her it was ok as usual and that I

4

had fun skateboarding. I asked again about my father and she said she had no idea where he was. I've never met my dad and would sometimes see my mom with other friends, but never really questioned any of it. I never missed not having a dad because he's never been there anyway.

As my mother stood up to leave my room, I called after her and yelled, "Love you mommy!"

She turned around with a huge smile, walked back towards me, gave me a bear hug and a kiss and said, "I love you to baby, good night."

When she left my room I said my prayers. I closed my eyes, thinking about the next day and about the needle I found in the bathroom. I wondered if I should have told my mother what I found or if I should have just given it to her. My instincts told me to put it in the trash because it was on the floor.

"Ah man!" I groaned.

CHAPTER TWO

There goes that alarm at six o'clock sharp. I always hated getting up in the morning, but once I was up I was good. I had my clothes and everything ready for school, so all I had to do was wash up and get dressed. My day was always the same: wake up, meet my friend Michael outside so we could walk to school together, and eat the candy we bought the day before. Sometimes I had candy and Michael didn't, and vice versa, but we always shared. On our way to school we would talk about the things we did yesterday or what we wanted to do that day. Sometimes I wondered if Michael had a good relationship with his parents and how things were at his home. I always knew, my mom didn't have much and would always piece things together as she went. It must feel good to have both parents around. There are some things I think of and would like to talk to my mother about, but I just don't know how to go about them. I know I can and she will listen, but how much do I really want to say to her? I'm just a kid.

"Mr. Johnson, do you have your homework?" Mrs. Hill asked.

"Yes ma'am," I answered

"Good, pass it down please."

Mrs. Hill is my teacher and she is always nice to me. I always wondered at times what other kids would think about when they would talk to me about things. Could it be that although I'm only nine, I think about things that a normal nine year old mind wouldn't? Maybe it's a good thing. Maybe I'm just different.

After lunch, I sat outside watching others play kickball, basketball, and everything else. I really didn't feel like playing any sports, so I sat and talked to some of the other kids who were probably thinking and feeling like I was. You know what they say; birds of a feather flock together.

On the other side of the yard a fight broke out and kids were all over the place chanting, "Get'em!"

I never liked being around trouble makers and never liked violence. The school principal and security guards broke up the fight and took the two kids that were fighting inside. I'm pretty sure they will get suspended for a week or two.

As we sat listening to the other kids talking about the fight, my friend Michael walked up to us with two of his friends. They immediately began making fun of one of the kid's sneakers that was with me. I've always tried to be a peace maker so I spoke up.

"That's not funny. Not everyone can afford name brand clothes."

I myself was one of them, although the clothes I wore were cool. Michael and his friends looked at me strangely, but stopped teasing the kid.

Trying to change the subject, Michael told me there was a girl that liked me and wanted him to give me a note. I paid him no mind because Michael is the class clown and sometimes tries to get me with his corny jokes. Besides, I was too young to be dating, but if I was, it would definitely be Lisa because she's pretty and always smells good.

Johnson smiled and thought to himself. *Smell good? You're only nine, what do you know about girls smelling good?*

Lisa was light skinned and had long hair. She wore glasses which made her look older than she was. I really liked her smile and the fact that she always talked to me whenever she got the chance. The bell finally rang, interrupting my thoughts of Lisa.

"Yes. Time to go!"

As I made my way down the crowded halls, I heard Michael calling me from a distance. "Johnson! Johnson, what's going on?"

"Not much man, just going home and maybe later my cousin Junior and I will go to Manhattan."

"Yeah that's right, it's Friday. You and Junior sometimes ride the trains to the ferry. Can I go with you guys?" Michael asked.

"It's your call Mike. We might get back a little later than our curfew. You might want to ask your parents if you can stay out an hour later," I suggested.

"Ok, I'll see you in a minute," said Michael.

I knew that on Friday or on the weekend I might get away with coming home an hour late. Even if I did get in trouble, to me it was worth it because Junior and I would sometimes come home with at least twenty to thirty dollars each from begging. That's right; we both would beg from the moment we got on the train in Brooklyn, to the boat, and back on the train on the way home. It's one, if not the biggest, thing my mother had no clue I was doing. If she knew what I was doing I would be in big trouble for a while and I knew it. It was one of the things I knew I should not be doing that my mom should know about, but I never said a word. It is things of this nature I felt made me different from other kids my age. I knew I was a good kid with a big heart, but what I didn't realize was that this was the beginning of trouble, manipulation, and dishonesty.

My cousin Junior lived about twenty minutes away by train. Junior's mother, MaryAnn, didn't know that Junior and I were going to Manhattan begging for money or she would have told my mother.

"Knock! Knock! Knock!"

I heard the door but wanted my mother to answer it so she wouldn't think I was up to no good by rushing to the door. Like clockwork, it was Junior. He was always the type to try different things. Junior was a little taller than me with a big head. I had no brothers or sisters, but Junior was close, like a brother to me. I knew he had my back and I had his. As we rushed down the stairs and out the door, my mother's friend Frank was entering the building. We said hello and kept going.

By the time we got off the train I must have had at least six dollars. Most of the time we would go under the turnstile at the train station and under at Bowling Green station. We loved riding on the ferry just to feel the wind blowing, see the beautiful sights, and over all, the excitement. It would take at least a half an hour to get to Staten Island by boat, and as always the Statue of Liberty was an amazing sight to see. Sometimes we would throw pennies into the ocean while others would be taking pictures, eating, and let's not forget about all the tourists coming to see the Statue of Liberty. By now Junior had about eighteen dollars and twenty five cents and I had twenty-two dollars and thirty four cents, so I wanted to head back home because I knew I was going to be about a half an hour to forty-five minutes late.

As I exited the "A" train, Junior waved and said, "See you later alligator," as the doors closed.

He's funny, I can see him laughing and making funny faces at me as the train pulled off.

CHAPTER THREE

"Boy, where you been?" Those were the first four words out my mother's mouth when I opened the door. She had company but it didn't matter, she was always on point when it came to me.

"I.....I went..." I started.

"Go to your room and I will deal with you later," she ordered.

About three minutes later mom called me and told me to go wash up, eat, and go back to my room. I knew I was in trouble. She wasn't going to embarrass me in front of company, but once they left and if I wasn't asleep by then, I would hear it. The sneaky part of me was saying at least I have enough money to buy candy and things from the store for the next week or so, but the big question was, what was my mother going to do this time? As I heard footsteps getting closer to my bedroom door, I closed my eyes and pretended to be asleep. My mother opened the door and looked at me for about five seconds and closed the door.

I wonder if she knew I was faking to be asleep.

She probably did because mothers know their children and I'm glad she left without punishing me, but tomorrow is when my mother will surely discipline me.

I woke up not to the sound of my alarm, but from my mother shaking me, saying get up so we could talk before she left. It was eight fifty-seven in the morning and I almost forgot about coming home late yesterday and was sure that's what this talk was going to be about.

"Son, you know I love you and don't want anything to happen to you, right?" she began.

"I know mom."

"Then why do you have me worrying about you by not coming home on time?"

"Mom, I'm sorry. Sometimes I have so much fun that the time flies by. I don't mean to be late intentionally and I'm willing to accept any and all punishment you give me."

"You are all I have and I don't know what I would do if something were to happen to you. I'm not going to punish you this time, but you won't get allowance for two weeks," she said sternly.

To me that was punishment, but she didn't know I had almost twenty-three dollars from yesterday. I've only gone to Manhattan about four times with Junior and it became almost like a game to get people to give us money. Maybe the fact that we're kids and used reasons like, 'we are trying to get home but don't have any money; or we're hungry and trying to get money for food', so people would give us money. Ninety percent of the time it would work. I don't know about Junior, but afterwards, and sometimes during, I would feel guilty because I was not raised to lie, cheat, or steal. I stashed twenty dollars in my hiding spot and put the rest in my dresser drawer. My mother never did tell me where she was going this morning, but would sometimes say things like 'she's going to see a man about a horse.' Other times, she'd say don't ask her where she's going and that she's the adult.

I really did try to keep track of her whereabouts because she's the true love of my life and I never had a clue where she would run off to at times. When I woke up my mother had not come home yet, but left a note on the refrigerator door telling me to take out the trash. I always liked helping my mother around the house. As I cleaned, I imagined buying my mother a big house and having a huge dog in the yard. I knew she would like that and she definitely deserved it. I can't wait to see my mom's friend Frank's dog. He has a huge white and grey Siberian husky. She makes me laugh sometimes when she barks because she sounds like she's trying to talk.

"All done!" I said to myself. "Nothing left to do but shower and play my video games."

As I stepped into the shower, I felt an asthma attack coming on.

"I have to find my pump. Where is that stupid asthma pump?" I yelled to no one.

As I get aggravated and frustrated, I now feel my asthma getting worse. My mother wasn't home and my wheezing and breathing is getting heavier. I tried to run hot water for steam, but that wasn't working. As soon as I turned off the faucet with tears in my eyes, I heard the sweet sound of a key sliding in the hole of the door.

"Mommy! Mommy!"

"What's wrong baby?" she yelled.

16

"I can't breathe. Where is my pump?" I wheezed.

"I put it in your dresser draw because you had it on the kitchen table. Sit here on the sofa."

She rushed back with my pump, feeling terrible as she watched me go through this. Normally, when my asthma gets bad I'm rushed to the hospital. Mom was hoping history wouldn't repeat itself. I pushed the pump three times and continued to breathe heavy as I sat on my mother's lap.

"Feeling better baby?" Mom asked.

"A little," I answered.

"Doesn't mommy always tell you to keep your asthma pump in one place? Either in your dresser or in your pocket so you know where to find it when you need it?" she lectured.

We had no home phone so I couldn't call anyone during one of my attacks, so my mother always had to make sure I had my pump or an alternative trip to the emergency room to get my shots if needed.

"Feeling better baby?" she asked again.

"Yes mom."

After about a minute or so of silence I said, "Mom? Can I ask you a question?"

"Yes honey, you can ask mommy anything you want." Parents know their children, but mom was unprepared for what I was about to ask her.

"Mom, I found a needle on the floor the other day in the bathroom and threw it away. What was the needle for and where did it come from?"

"Listen son, you're a little young to know about this. I was keeping it a secret, but I guess the secret is out," she sighed. "The needle is for heroin users and is a tool needed to inject heroin."

When she told me this I was confused. "Mom, you use drugs?"

"Yes I do, sweetie. I'm sorry you found out the way you did but know that mommy loves you and always will."

I heard in school and in conversations on the street about drugs and people that used them. I knew drugs were bad and sometimes killed the people who used them.

"Mom, do you like drugs?"

I knew mom wanted to change the conversation, but she knew I was persistent and until I totally understood what was going on, I would ask question after question.

"Yes," she replied. "Yes, but I'm seeking help and trying to stop."

After she said that I felt a little better, but a tear streamed down the left side of my cheek and I tried to hide it beneath my mother's arms. Moments later, I thought that now would be a good time to talk to mom about the train rides, ferry, and the begging; all of which I knew I was not allowed to do. I felt if mom could come clean about her heroin use, then I should also come clean about my sneakiness.

"Mom, can I tell you something?"

"Yes baby, go ahead."

"Mom I know you're going to be upset, but you said I could talk to you about anything. Mom, Junior and I went to Manhattan about four times by ourselves."

"What!?" she said, with a look of surprise on her face.

"We sneak onto the trains and the turnstile at Bowling Green and get on the ferry to beg for money. We did it more so for fun than the money."

"And you ain't bring mommy no money back?" she laughed, joking. "But seriously son, I try very hard to give you what you need and more, so there's no need for that."

Although my mother had her problems, she was pretty much on point when it came to providing for me. Most mothers would do anything to make sure their child had what they needed by any means. She was highly upset and sent me to my room. As I pretended to shut my door, I could see the pain I had caused. My mother and I went to church every Sunday and tomorrow was one Sunday service I hoped to attend. Church would always make mom and I feel better and we both needed a lift due to all the drama these last few days.

CHAPTER FOUR

It's Sunday morning and we're on our way to Sunday school. We paid our way onto the train and sat down. Looking at my mother, I saw myself and smiled at the fact that she looks just like me, but a woman version. She looked at me and smiled back as if she knew my thoughts. An old lady looked at us both as if she could see the unconditional love we both shared. At least that's what my thoughts were of what she was thinking.

After service, we left hand to hand to McDonalds, my favorite. I knew we wouldn't order much, but anything from Mickey Dee's was fine with me. As we left McDonalds, the conversation of what I wanted to be when I grew up was mentioned. I told my mom that I always liked helping people, so whatever trade I take, it must include helping people in a big way.

My mother grinned and said, "Why you don't become a clown because you act silly all the time."

I laughed and responded with, "I am silly, but strong in many areas, especially when it comes to defending my mommy."

We all know some kids pretend to be strong in strength, but in my mind I was as strong as I wanted to be. As we walked to the corner store I realized I had a few dollars left from the money I was given several days ago. My mother looked at me as if she knew this was some of the money I was given from begging. Once inside the store I brought candy, a soda, and asked my mother if she wanted anything.

"Yeah baby, you can buy mommy a house and get a maid to clean up after you," she laughed.

I laughed hysterically. "Mom when I get older I'm going to buy you the world and everything in it."

I told my mother I had ten dollars for her. She was shocked. "My son is giving me money at age nine?"

As we reached home, I quickly ran up the stairs and took two five dollar bills out of my shoe box to give to my mother. As I handed her the money, she looked at me with joy in her eyes.

"Mommy knows you mean well, but keep this money for yourself."

She told me to spend it wisely because we were struggling with bills and all. As I headed to my room to prepare for bed, I heard a knock at the door. My mother told me to answer the door, but to ask who it was first.

"Ok! Mom, its auntie MaryAnn."

"Open the door for her."

"Hello handsome," Aunt MaryAnn greeted me, lightly tapping me on my head.

"Hey Aunty."

"Where is your mother?"

"She's in her room. She'll be out in a minute."

"Mom!" I yelled.

"Ok boy, I'm coming, I'm coming," she said as she made her way down the stairs. "What's up girl?" she greeted Aunt Mary Ann.

"Not much, just stopped by to talk to you about Junior's behavior."

"What about him?" mom asked, with a look of concern.

"Well let me start by saying he's failing in school, has a smart mouth, and the thirty-six dollars I found in a sock in his dresser drawer."

"Thirty-six dollars? Johnson and I had a talk the other day and he did mention something about him and Junior going to Manhattan four or five times to beg for money."

"They did what?!" MaryAnn asked in surprise.

"Yes, I was going to put Johnson on punishment or even spank him, but instead I took away his allowance for two weeks."

"Those boys are crazy," MaryAnn said, shaking her head. "They could have been hurt, even killed out there!"

"I know, I know," mom sighed.

"Not only that Renay, but Junior is getting D's and F's in school and will probably get left back. I told him to clean his room and do the dishes, and he told me, "Not now, wait a minute.""

"He said what?" mom said, clearly surprised.

I overheard the conversation about Junior from my room and couldn't believe he was being so disrespectful to my aunt. I myself never really liked school, but knew my mother would never allow me to get D's and F's. Not my mom. I wonder if my mother ever looked at me as being disrespectful to her. I don't think so, but other people may see things in us we don't see in ourselves, so we must always be careful of what we say to others so we don't disrespect them or hurt their feelings.

Although Junior was older than me and sometimes seemed smarter, we needed to have to have a serious talk. There was school tomorrow, so I took a shower and finished up a spider man art work I had started. I wonder what happened to Michael. He never came back to go with me and Junior to Manhattan. I'm sure I'll see him in school tomorrow. Besides, I don't think I'll be going back to Manhattan with Junior any more.

As I woke up to my Mickey Mouse alarm clock ringing, I heard my mother's voice yelling for me to get up. I must have fallen back to sleep after the first ring. "I'm up mom, I'm up," I groaned.

I smelled eggs and toast as soon as I opened my room door. For some reason, I knew today was unlike any other day. Although my mother would sometimes surprise me with gifts, today was my birthday and she would always start it off right.

"Happy birthday!" she yelled. I immediately looked at her as if I thought she'd forgotten this very special day.

"You thought I forgot your birthday, right?"

"No. How could you ever forget your one and only sweet, kind, and loving son's birthday?"

"Take these forty dollars and later when you come home from school we will do something special."

"Thanks mom, I love you so much!"

"I know, I love you too baby!"

By now I was feeling really good. I had about sixty dollars and my mother was happy so today was starting off just great.

"I think I will buy my mother something with this money I have, she deserves it," I said to myself.

As soon as I opened the front door Michael was sitting on my door step asking, "What took you so long man, we are going to be late for school."

I knew we were about five minutes behind schedule, and we always stopped at the candy store to buy candy. I already had a lot of candy so I knew we weren't going to be late.

"Happy birthday!" Michael said to me.

"Thanks man."

On our way to school I showed Michael the amount of money I had. "Wow where did you get all that money?" Michael asked.

"Some of it's from going to Manhattan, and my mother gave me forty dollars for my birthday this morning."

"Man, you're rich!"

"You have any money?" I asked.

"Nah, my parents are kind of strapped for cash at the present time."

"Here's three dollars," I offered, handing him the money.

"Thank you Johnson, I'll pay it back when I can."

"You don't have to, that's what friends are for. I know you would do the same for me, right Michael?"

"Yep, because you're my friend."

"Johnson, I'm sorry I didn't come back to let you know if I was going to Manhattan with you and Junior the other day."

"It's ok Mike. Guess what Junior did?"

"What?"

"He told his mother to wait when she told him to do the dishes and clean his room."

"You're kidding me right?"

"Nope!"

"Wow! I know your Aunt MaryAnn was very hurt by that."

"Yeah, Junior and I will definitely talk about that. He's my cousin and all, but I don't appreciate him disrespecting my aunt like that. He's also getting D's and F's."

"Man our parents would never allow that!" he said, surprised.

"I know. I won't be going to Manhattan anymore."

CHAPTER FIVE

After school, I wanted to get my mother something nice, but something from the corner store wasn't going to do. I had to try to get to a dollar store or something, or use reverse psychology to get my mother to take me. I didn't want to sneak to the store after admitting to going to Manhattan with Junior several times and because of all the pain I had caused mom. As soon as I opened the door I heard, "Surprise!" There was a brand new Huffy dirt bike parked in the living room.

"Thanks mom!"

"You're welcome baby."

"I always wanted one of these!" I said happily. "Can I go out to ride mom?"

"Not just yet, you have to do your homework first then you and mommy will go somewhere special," she answered.

"Ok mom."

I took my new bike into my bedroom to look at it while I did my homework. I never really had a hard time doing my homework, but this new bike staring at me made it difficult. "Mom, I'm all done."

"Okay, give me a minute baby. Alright this is good, this is good, but you have to remember to carry over the extra number when it's over ten."

"Ok mom, now where are we going because I want to ride in the wind!" I said excitedly.

"Relax silly boy," mom laughed. "Now go get your jacket because it may get a little windy." While on the train I thought about going to Manhattan, unaware that was our destination. "Mom this is the train Junior and I take to Manhattan."

"I know."

I reached inside my pants pocket and pulled out a pack of banana flavored Now and Laters.

"Boy you are not going to have any teeth by the time your thirty."

"Mom, I'm missing about three teeth now," I giggled, revealing three missing teeth.

"That's because you're only nine and they have not come in yet."

As we paid to enter the ferry's turnstile, mom looked at the ferry to see the amount of people waiting to get on. She looked at the ship to see how it was docked while the captain called for passengers to board the ferry. We moved closer to get on. I know by now my mother was feeling the rush I felt the first time I rode the ferry. As we pulled off, you could feel the boat bumping the side walls it was docked at. The captain sounded the ship's horn as we pulled out into the ocean. As the ship speed reached approximately eight knots, we felt the wind blowing and the open sea looking quite inviting.

"This is so beautiful," mom said to me.

"Isn't it mom?"

Although my mother and I have done plenty of things together, we have never experienced anything of this nature before. I pulled out some change to give to my mother.

"Mom, this is what we do sometimes with the coins," I said, throwing a dime into the ocean. Junior and I never threw quarters or dimes in the ocean, but this was a special occasion so it was well worth it.

"Throw this in mom, but make a wish before you do."

I went first. First, I wished for my mother and I to have many more good times, happiness, and a better relationship together. Before my mother threw her coins out to sea, she prayed and wished to stop her heroin use, to love me the best she could, and to keep me out of harm's way and safe.

"Look mom! Do you see the Statue of Liberty way over there?"

"Yes baby."

"And over there is where the Twin Towers once stood."

Mom looked as if she was really enjoying the sights, the breeze and the seagulls that looked as if they were following the ship for food. As we both stood with our hands on the ships railing, my mom put one of her arms around me as if for protection. I was pleased that my mother surprised me by taking me to the ferry. I would have loved to go with her before, minus the begging part. I knew it wasn't by coincidence my mother took me to Manhattan, but in fact a blessing because it brought us closer. I knew when I talked to Junior I could use a bad experience and turn it into a good one. It was then I realized that everything that seemed bad wasn't, and many incidents are simply a learning experience.

When we arrived home, Junior was sitting at the top step of our apartment building. He looked kind of troubled. As soon as my mom asked him what was wrong he started crying hysterically. As we walked into the house I asked my mother if I could talk to Junior on the porch. I knew this would be the perfect time to talk to him about his attitude and behavior issues.

"Sure, but don't leave because it's getting dark out."

"Ok mom. Junior, what's going on?"

"A whole lot man, my mother and I got into it because she feels as though I have been disrespectful, dishonest, and my grades have been going downhill."

Junior needs the kind of tough love my mother has been known to give me at times.

"Junior, you must respect your mother at all times," I began. "We have done things that were wrong at times, but our parents are all we have. And what's up with your grades man? I heard you're getting D's and F's."

Junior looked at me as if he was surprised at the tone of my voice and facial expression.

I continued, "I looked up to you because of the person you are and because you're older than me. You're my cousin and I want us both to be smart and to lead by example. I can't hang out with you if you're going to be disrespectful to Aunty like that. I told my mom that we have been going to Manhattan to beg for money."

"You did what!?" snapped Junior.

"I had to. I don't like lying to my mother. She forgave me and even took me to Manhattan on the ferry for my birthday, which is today."

"That's right, happy birthday."

"Thank you. See Junior, sometimes you can turn a bad situation into a good one, but first you must identify what it is and work to change it."

Junior decided to make a deal with me. "If I promise to respect my mother more and do better in school, will you help me with some of my homework to improve my grades?"

"Deal!" I agreed.

Junior looked at me with a smirk on his face and said, "I guess this means no more ferry rides, huh?"

"Nope!" We both laughed.

"Come on Junior lets go inside. By now my mom would like to know what's going on, and you know she's going to want to take you home because it's getting dark."

"Okay."

While on the train, mom, Junior, and I had a very good talk. Mom explained to Junior how he hurt his mother by his choices and the way he was living.

"The same way I feel about Johnson is the same way MaryAnn feels about you," she informed him.

As we all talked about the important things in life, I realized there was a lot to learn; I realized I was maturing fast and wanted to make sure I could talk to my mother about anything. Junior lived in a tall building and life was pretty good for him and his family. They lived on the sixteenth floor, apartment 316 and had most of the finer things in life. When Aunty MaryAnn opened the door she was surprised to see the three of us standing there, especially since Junior has been missing for the last four hours.

"Hey girl. Boy where have you been all this time?!" she yelled.

Mom took control of the situation. "Let's all sit down and talk," she suggested, trying to calm the situation.

I knew this conversation was going to be good and was pleased to see a negative turn into a positive.

"When we arrived home Junior was sitting at our door step crying," Mom began. "We all had a good conversation on the train and this situation needs to be dealt with. These kids are too young to be riding the trains alone, and as their parents we need to know their whereabouts and problems."

Aunty MaryAnn looked at me, back at Junior and said, "Yes, you're absolutely right. I try very hard to raise this boy the best I can, but I can try a little harder because I refuse to lose my son to the streets."

"Now get up and give your son a nice big hug before my handsome son and I leave to go home," mom smiled.

After that very emotional moment, mommy said, "I like what you did to the apartment since the last time we visited you."

"Oh thank you girl, I try. Okay girl, you guys get home safe. Junior and I have some catching up to do before his father gets home."

I exhaled as we got on the elevator.

CHAPTER SIX

On the train ride home I rested my head on my mother's lap and suddenly remembered my new Huffy waiting for me at home. I knew it was going to be too late to ride, but tomorrow I was going to burn rubber. As I woke up to the beeping sound of the train door opening, I felt my mother pulling me to get up.

"Come on baby, this is our stop."

On the way home I thought about the responsibilities I have as a young man. I realized that even a nine year old has responsibilities that parents expect of them. I thought about how all parents were kids at one point of their life and dealt with issues such as myself. At that very moment and time in my life, I came to the conclusion that I was thinking responsibly and decided to challenge things head on.

On my way to school the next day I saw a man lying on the sidewalk covered up in a dirty blanket. Although I was young, I knew he was homeless and probably had no money. I reached in my pocket and gave him three of the five dollars I had. My mother always told me to never deny anyone food and to help people whenever possible. I was going to wake him up, but instead folded the money and put it under his blanket with two packs of Now and Laters, banana and strawberry flavored; my favorite. As I reached half way down the block the homeless man stood up and began to fold his blanket. I watched him as the money and Now and Laters fell to the ground. Although I was a good distance away, it looked as if he smiled as he ate one of the candies. I wanted him to at least be able to eat something this morning. I thought if I was in his situation I would like and appreciate if someone did the same for me. When I finally made it to school I saw Mrs. Hill in the hallway.

"Hello Mrs. Hill."

"Hello Mr. Johnson. How was your weekend? Happy belated birthday!"

"Thank you ma'am. It was okay and I learned quite a bit over the weekend. Oh, and I got a new Huffy dirt bike!"

She asked how I was doing in my math class and I told her it was coming along, but I still needed improvement in certain areas. I told her sometimes I get caught up looking at so many numbers when multiplying or dividing. Mrs. Hill told me to take my time and think things out. She said there is a format in all maths and once I know them I will be ok. I'm going to do some reading, I kept thinking to myself on my way home. I know that reading is fundamental and also helps improve one's vocabulary.

Is that Lisa at the corner? Yes that's her. I know she hasn't noticed me yet because she always makes it her business to speak to me when she sees me. My heart always beats fast when I see her. Could this be puppy love?

"Hello Johnson," said Lisa, finally speaking.

"Hello Lisa."

"How was your weekend, and by the way, happy belated birthday. What did you get for your birthday?"

"For starters, I got a new Huffy dirt bike."

"Yeah? So now you can give me a ride or even ride me to school one day."

Is she joking?

"Lisa, you can definitely ride my bike all by yourself."

Lisa smiled at me as if she knew I liked her.

I smiled back. "Ok Lisa, I'm turning here, see you later alligator. Oh wait a minute Lisa, you think you can help me study math?" I asked. I knew Lisa was an A student and wouldn't mind helping me if she could.

"Sure Johnson, let me get all my math material together and maybe we can meet up tomorrow."

"That's fine. Hey Lisa, make sure you let your parents know where you're at, ok? "

"Mom you home?" I yelled as I walked through the door.

"Yes baby, I'm in the kitchen."

"Mom, have you seen my book, *'What About Johnson?'* I brought it home from the library the other day."

"No, I told you that you are responsible for your own belongings, but I think I saw it on top of the refrigerator. Check there."

"I got it mom."

What About Johnson?

I never really liked reading much, but this book, 'What About Johnson?' was pretty good and reminded me of myself. The book I was reading was only sixty-something pages.

"That looks like a really good book you're reading baby. How was school today?" Mom asked.

"It was fine. I gave some homeless man three dollars this morning on my way to school. I also gave him two packs of Now and Laters."

"Why did you do that son?"

"Honestly, I really don't know why, I just thought of it and did it."

"That's great baby. Son, we as people have these things called instincts; instincts are a part of a person's brain that tells them to do something before they think about it clearly enough."

She told me I would be blessed for it. I didn't know what blessed meant, but I knew it meant something good. After reading and doing my homework, I decided to ride in the wind. My bike was all red with grey lettering. Before I could even get on the bike, I heard my mother yell, "Don't leave that bike unattended!"

To me the neighborhood I lived in wasn't bad, but I was only ten and haven't been around to see much yet.

"Ok mom."

As I rode up and down the block I wanted to venture off a little, so I decided to ride around the neighborhood. Riding was so much more fun than walking. I saw the world as if on tour. The other kids in the neighborhood were looking at me as if I was the main attraction. I knew Junior, Lisa, and Michael would be the only ones I let ride. After seeing bicycles chained up to poles with wheels and parts missing, my instincts told me to invest in a security chain. The fact that I'm ten years old now, I knew that in a few more years I would be taking on greater responsibilities. At ten, I felt I was being led by a powerful positive force that constantly reminded me to treat people as I wanted to be treated, but more importantly, I desperately sought attention but was too afraid to let others in my circle. *I'm beat, I'm going home to eat and relax.*

"I'm home mom!" I yelled as I walked through the door.

"Ok baby, take your bicycle and chain it up in the hallway."

"Mom this girl named Lisa is supposed to study with me tomorrow. She's going to help me with my math."

"That's great. So you got yourself a girlfriend I see," she teased.

"No mom, I'm too young for a girlfriend, but she is pretty."

"Ok, go clean up and get ready for dinner."

"Mom, do you know how to dance?"

"Sure I can dance a little, why you ask?"

"Because I've never seen you dance before. In fact, I hardly ever see you enjoying yourself or laughing much."

Mom replied, "I laugh and joke with you all the time silly."

"Yeah mom, but I mean a really good laugh when tears come to your eyes or like watching a movie or something funny and burst out laughing hysterically."

"That's funny because you don't laugh much either, so maybe we are alike." Mom told me people have different characteristics and some do things more than others.

"I understand."

As I lay on my bed slowly falling asleep to the sound of my window fan, I heard what seemed to be sounds of whispering. I knew mother and I were alone and was curious to know where it was coming from. When I opened my room door to look around, I saw my mother on her knees crying and praying asking God to help her stay strong, get clean, and to protect her son. I listened to her pray for about a minute or so before I went in the living room to sit by her side. As I rubbed her back she looked up at me with tears in her eyes and said, "Thank you baby, now go to bed, you have school tomorrow."

CHAPTER SEVEN

There's nothing like waking up to a big breakfast. French toast, eggs and bacon, and a nice cold glass of orange juice.

"Good morning handsome, slept good last night?" Mom asked.

"Yes mom."

"Ok, hurry and wash up so you don't be late for school."

Today was a big day for me. After school I had to study with Lisa, do my homework, and peddle in the wind on my new bike. Michael hadn't seen my new bike yet and I couldn't wait to show it to him. As soon as I opened my front door there he was.

"Hey Johnson! Whose bike is this?" He asked.

"It's my bike. Come on Michael, we're going to be late for school. Lisa and I are supposed to study today after school. I'm trying to catch up on my math and Lisa is definitely the person to help me. "

Michael looked at me and said, "And she's pretty too!"

We both laughed. On the way to school I explained to Michael, Junior's outcome and other things I had going on in my life. Michael looked surprised at how hectic my life seemed to be. He warned me that at age ten, I will have many obstacles and I will have to pick and choose my battles. At that moment I knew our conversation was on an adult level and that we were good friends indeed.

At lunch time I had to look for Lisa to find out what time we would meet. Today I have a science test that I need to score at least an eighty-five to pass that subject. When I looked over my shoulder, Lisa and two of her girlfriends were walking towards Michael and me. They sat down next to us.

"Five thirty." she smiled.

Her two friends looked at me as if they knew we were studying today. "Ok Lisa, I will be there waiting for you."

She looked at me as her long, jet black hair swung from side to side. As she walked away I said to Michael,

"She's beautiful. One day I will have a girlfriend as gorgeous as her."

As Michael and I headed to class, I rushed to my locker to put away my extra books, but kept the book, *'What About Johnson?'* with me. I just couldn't put that book down once I started reading it, and that's good coming from someone who doesn't like reading much. As I sat in science class taking my test, I remembered my mom praying, so I asked God to help my mother in all she does. Although the test was important, it was the first time I experienced a prayer that meant so much. I couldn't wait to study with Lisa and get home to my bike that kept calling me in class during my test. On my way home, I thought about helping Junior with his studies. I myself needed help with my work, but I was determined to help because at some point in life we all need help with something.

On my way upstairs I looked at my bike to make sure it was safe and secured. As soon as I got near the door, I heard voices coming from my apartment. When I opened the door I saw the lady of my dreams; it was Lisa.

"But how--" I was shocked and totally caught off guard. "What are you---I mean, how did you get here before me Lisa?"

"Well Johnson, when you were leaving school my friend Sheila and I stayed about a block and a half away to beat you home. I knew you would be surprised, but that was my plan. That's why my friends were smiling at you in the lunch room. "

"You're funny Lisa."

Mom was smiling, but deep down she knew I was embarrassed, but happy Lisa was in my presence.

"Ok, I'm going to leave you both to study," mom said.

There was milk, cookies, and chocolate cake on the table my mom prepared for us. I thought this was great. I'm studying and on a date at the same time. Yes! As Lisa pulled out her books, notes, and calculator, she explained that I must first learn the formats. She said formats mean more or less the way you do things to get the correct results. She smelled like strawberry lotion. We sat about two and a half feet away. She looked at me at times as if she were looking straight through me. As I was almost about to panic, she said "No, first you must make sure all your numbers are lined up and counted. You must also know your multiplication table to be able to do math, it is the first step you must master before moving on. "

After Lisa and I were done she asked if I liked school. "Not all subjects, but I will do what I have to do to graduate and get my high school diploma," I answered.

"That's great, because school is the key to success and prayer will help in any area or problem that may arrive in life," she responded.

Just when Lisa was walking out the door, my big headed cousin, Junior, was about to ring the door bell. "Hi Junior," Lisa greeted him.

"Hi Lisa," Junior replied.

I looked at Junior as if to say, "See, this is what life is all about." It was perfect timing, because Junior needed to see he wasn't the only one that needed help with his school work. "Ok Lisa, I will see you later."

"Ok. Bye Johnson, practice makes perfect," she reminded me.

"Come on in big head," I said to Junior.

As Junior and I studied, I think Junior knew this was the example needed to become productive and respectful. My mother always said some people need a little push and they will be fine. Junior asked me what I wanted to be when I grow up.

"I'm not sure yet, but maybe an artist or a singer / song writer."

He told me he was thinking of being a police officer or doctor. I told him in order to become successful, we must first respect others and listen to our parents so we will be strong, able to lead, and guide others in their time of need.

"I want to be like you when I grow up," Junior said.

"First, your head has to be shrunken down in size," I teased.

Junior hit me on the shoulder and said, "Good one."

After we studied for about an hour and a half, Junior told me he's not going to be around people who are a bad influence. He doesn't want to get in trouble anymore and it stops here and now. I told him I understood because my mom talks to me all the time about making the right choices. I explained that like him, I sometimes think of things that are not right.

"Junior let me tell you something that will make the hairs on your head stand up." I was referring to my mother's drug use, my thoughts about dealing with my own problems, and my negative behaviors and attitude.

"Junior, I sometimes feel like telling my mother things but don't, because I don't know how to let it out or express my inner childhood emotions, thinking she wouldn't understand. I sometimes feel like I'm wearing a mask; not physically, but mentally. I shelter my deepest feelings that truly need to be expressed and exposed. It can be painful, plus harmful, if we do not talk about them to others who are concerned about our well being. You have parents that love and care for you, so you should utilize that and stay connected to your family's values, love, cares, and concerns. It will be all you will need to mature as a man and to be responsible and independent."

As a tear appeared on Junior's cheek, he replied, "I love you cousin."

While Junior and I studied, he realized that we shared some of the same hidden feelings. We never talked about things that had to do with life's issues so we could definitely identify with each other.

"Junior, your time is up. We'll continue with this some other time." I was now committed to helping Junior to the end because now we had a stronger bond than ever before.

As Junior left to go home mom said to me, "Did I ever tell you that you have a step-brother named Gee?"

"No mom. How old is he?"

"He's your age and lives with your father and his wife somewhere."

Mom said she never met him, but we will meet some time next year if possible. I was pleased to know that somewhere out there was a step-brother I would one day meet.

CHAPTER EIGHT

After I completed my homework, I began to read *'What About Johnson?'* until I fell asleep. That night I dreamed about homeless people fighting over food and old clothing. I remember talking in my sleep, telling them to stop fighting and there was enough food for everyone. After waking up with tears in my eyes, I knew I wanted to make a difference in the world. I was now starting to think positive. How I was going to accomplish my goals and dreams was starting to manifest in my young mind. That morning I asked my mother why the world was so corrupt and angry.

"I notice how the world is so aggressive and mean mom." Mom told me everyone is not bad, but that's simply the way it is. She said that's why she's so over protective with me, because she recognizes anything is possible and there are many dangerous people out there. She told me to always think of the choices I make before I act them out. I asked my mother about death.

"Mom, where do people go when they die?"

"There are many religions out there and some people believe your soul goes to heaven or hell. It depends on what your belief is."

I thought quietly for a moment. "I want to go to heaven because that's where God sits with his son and all his angels."

Mom smiled at me. "Me too baby, mommy does too."

I wanted to go to the park and asked if I could go. Mom said to make sure my room was clean and to do the dishes before I left. At the park, three kids were playing basketball that I had never seen before, so I sat on the bleachers and watched them play. I always had difficulties meeting and greeting people. As I sat and observed them, one of the boys looked at me and smiled. I didn't pay it much attention, but smiled back because mom always told me to be polite. Seconds later, one of the boys approached me asking me my name.

"Johnson, my name is Johnson," I said, introducing myself. He said his name was Greg but his friends called him Gee. I asked him what they were playing. Greg told me they were playing horse and explained the way the game is played.

"I've seen people playing the game but never played it myself," I informed him.

"My two friends wanted to know if you wanted to play a two on two," Gee offered.

I was never a basketball player, or played on a team, but thought I'd give it a try. Before we started to play, I felt as though I was out of place and didn't belong. I felt as though I was in a small world alone with three strangers. I knew this was what I needed to open up to others and a possible friendship with three people I've never met before. Gee and I were on the same team and played against the other two. As we began to play, I wondered if I would make a fool out of myself. As Gee took the ball out, he began to shuffle the ball between his legs and behind his back. As I watched Gee's most fascinating moves, I wasn't ready for what was about to happen. While I was looking at his fancy footwork, Gee threw the ball to me, hitting me in the face with the ball.

"Ahh!" I screamed. I now had my hands covering my face and was in so much pain. Everyone stopped in their tracks and walked over to me.

"You ok?" Gee asked with concern.

For about twenty seconds everything was silent. I removed my hands from my face with tears in both eyes and a huge red swelling mark. "Yeah, I'm fine," I answered. I knew my mother would inquire about the mark on my face, but I was committed to completing this game. "I'm no quitter. Let's play."

Now that all the attention was on my face, I guess they all were thinking this boy is tough because most kids would have run home crying to one of their parents.

"Ya'll ready?" I asked.

"Yeah, let's play!" they all yelled.

I only weighed about eighty-three pounds but I was strong for my age. Every time I got the ball I would dribble with my right hand. I didn't have much control with my left hand, but with my right hand no one could take the ball away. The score was twenty-one to eleven. Gee and I had won the game. Even with a sore face, I felt better I had won the game. It helped build my confidence and boost my ego a little.

"I have to go now, but I will try to make it out here again to play with you guys." I asked them what school they all went to and they all said P.S. 138 in Brooklyn. "I go to that school too, but never seen you guys there before! Okay, I'll see ya'll later. Take care."

On my way home I thought about the name, Gee. *My mom said I have a brother by that name.* I didn't think about it too long as I walked home with my face still in pain.

"What happened to your face?" Those were the first words out of my mother's mouth when I walked into the house. She told me to sit down as she rushed to look at my face. I sat on the sofa as my mom pressed a cold towel with crushed ice in it on my face.

"Mom, I'm okay. I was playing basketball at the park and was hit in the face with the ball. I should have been looking at the ball instead of Gee with all his fancy Michael Jordan moves. It won't happen again."

"I never knew you had friends that played basketball at the park on Saint Mark's."

"Mom, I just met them and we played a game."

"You're growing fast baby." She said she expects certain things like this to happen to me because I am a boy, and boys do play rough at times and get hurt. "Do you remember when you asked me about that thing you found in the bathroom?"

"Yes mom, I remember."

"You don't have to worry about that anymore because mommy is getting help and will always be there for you."

"Thanks mom."

As I lay on my bed with freezing cold ice on my face, I thought about the next basketball game and what moves I was going to make on them. I knew I wasn't as good as Gee but if I played hard I would fit in and make new friends.

That night my mother's friend, Frank, came over with a puppy his dog Sheba had given birth to. The puppy was white and brown, with a black streak alongside its right leg. I asked my mother if I could keep him, but she told me I couldn't take care of him like he needed to be taken care of. After begging and pleading with my mom, she gave in, telling me the minute I neglected the dog he would go straight to the pound. I wasn't about to let that happen because I was now learning what it meant to be responsible. The right side of my face was now being distracted by this cute little puppy that kept looking at me like, "well, what are we going to do now?" I cuddled with my little friend thinking of a good name to call him.

"I got it, I'll call him Bloopers. Yeah that's it, Bloopers!"

As Bloopers and I played and ran around my room, my mom and her friend Frank left and came back with a dog chain, a bed, and food for the dog. I tried to take a nap, only to be awoken by Bloopers, whining and barking for my attention. I could not sleep. *Is this what it's going to be like having a dog?* I got up to tend to Bloopers, putting him in the bed with me. He was clean and had all his shots, so it wasn't a problem. A few minutes later Bloopers and I were sound asleep.

I was awakened by my mother to eat dinner. It was right on time because I was exhausted from playing basketball and playing with the dog. McDonalds was what they brought back to eat and we all know how much I love

McDonalds. After eating, I fed Bloopers and took him for a walk. He was very small and didn't want to walk, so I pulled on his chain a little and he followed me like a cat chasing tuna. After Bloopers was done peeing and pooping, behind me stood Lisa.

"Hi Johnson," Lisa smiled.

"Hello Lisa."

"Is this your dog?"

"Yes. I just got him today."

"Aww, he's adorable! How old is he?"

"He's about one month old."

"Aww!"

I saw how much Lisa liked the puppy and asked her if she wanted to hold him for a while.

"Sure!" she said excitedly.

As Lisa and I stood talking about the dog, I asked, "So when are you coming over to help me with my homework again and to share some of those chocolate cookies?"

She said she could come over next week, but she had to check with her parents first.

"Okay," I said.

"Have you been studying?" she asked.

"Yes I have," I answered.

Lisa asked if I could keep a secret and that not even her closest friends knew what she was about to tell me. "I won't tell anyone, I promise," I said.

She paused for about four seconds; "I like you. Johnson I have liked you for a while but wasn't sure if I should say anything. I know we are too young to be boyfriend and girlfriend, but I thought I would tell you anyway. Even my girlfriends at school thought I liked you but couldn't figure me out."

I was shocked! For about twenty seconds I couldn't say a word. My heart was beating about a hundred times a minute and I couldn't just walk away because Lisa was still holding Bloopers, so that was out of the question.

"That's just great because I like you too but wasn't going to say anything either," I admitted.

So now that I know Lisa likes me are we going steady? In the back of my mind I heard my mother's voice saying loud and clear, "No!"

"Lisa, I will talk to you later because I have to take Bloopers back inside."

"Sure," said Lisa.

As soon as Lisa was out of my view, I pumped my fist and shouted out, "Yes!"

"Mommy! Mommy! Lisa likes me!"

"She does?" Mom asked, surprised.

"Yes, she told me when I was walking Bloopers."

"You're too young for a girlfriend boy."

"I know mom," I groaned.

Frank called me over to talk to me about girls. I sat on the armrest of the chair. "Yes, you are too young to have a girlfriend, but it's natural to have feelings at the age of ten," he lectured. "You will have time for girls later, but for now what's important is your schoolwork and listening to your mother, and oh, don't forget about your little buddy Bloopers."

Frank told me he understood how I felt because he was young once, and Lisa will be there when that time comes. Mom stood in silence and listened. Even though Frank wasn't my father, I guess he knew it was time to step up to the plate.

"Interesting," said Mom. "Now, go to your room and play while Frank and I talk."

CHAPTER NINE

I walked to my room thinking about all that happened to me today. I sat on my bed with absolutely nothing to do. I decided to finish reading the book, 'What About Johnson?' I had twelve pages left and I wanted to know how Johnson turned out in the end. It was the kind of book I would definitely recommend to a friend. After reading about seven pages, I fell asleep with Bloopers at the end of the bed.

Ring! Ring!

My alarm went off, but today was Saturday and I forgot to turn it off. Now that I was up, I decided to feed the dog and take him for a walk. "What's this?" I said out loud, noticing the wet spot on my bed.

I looked under Blooper's belly and realized the dog had wet the bed. I knew the dog was not allowed to sleep on my bed, but I was tired of the barking and whining. I was going to tell my mother, but after I changed the sheets.

That darn dog! He's going to be sleeping in his doggy bed from now on.

I didn't know how to train a dog but I did my best. Well at least I don't have to walk him for now, but I still need to feed him.

"Mom, Bloopers wet the bed."

"How did he wet the bed when he should always be on the floor?"

"I let him sleep with me yesterday because he kept barking, so; I picked him up to sleep with me so he would stop."

"Ok, but from now on let him sleep in his own bed so he can get used to it."

"Mom, I can't wait to see my step-brother, and do you think Junior is listening to Aunty MaryAnn?"

"As for your step-brother, I don't know when that will happen, but I hope it happens soon because you need to know your siblings." She sighed. "Junior is doing well from what Aunty Ann said. The last time I spoke to her she said Junior is doing all his homework and is following up on his chores, only time will tell for sure baby."

"I have to help him. Although I'm in need of help with my own homework, I need to be there and help him with his. He's my cousin and I must return the favor."

"Yeah, because your pretty friend Lisa is helping you," mom giggled. She pulled me by the arm started to tickle me.

"Stop mom! You're going to make me pee my pants!" I said between laughs.

"Oh, like Bloopers did on your bed?" she chuckled.

I started laughing hysterically. I looked very much my mom, and every time we bonded my mother told me she would think about when her baby was just a baby. We loved each other so much that nothing could ever come between us. I was a mommy's boy, but was growing up fast into a young man. I would always open the doors for my elders and was very helpful around the house. I was the kind of young man who would seek answers within me before asking others around me. I would sometimes make and build things just to tear them apart and rebuild them again. Sometimes I would sit for hours trying to perfect my ideas. I was pretty good with my hands and would only show my mother or Michael my work. I was also the quietest student in my class. Mrs. Hill, my teacher, always told me that one day I would be someone great. Mrs. Hill worked with children for over thirty something years, so she could kind of tell what kind of child she was working with, although some kids change with time.

I had school tomorrow, so after my homework and chores around the house I would relax. I thought about riding my bicycle, but now that I have Bloopers I would spend some time with him to bond and love. That night I thought about my friend Michael. I wanted to see him to talk about all that has been going on in the last few days or so. I would make it my business to see Michael in school tomorrow. The next morning I was awakened not by my noisy alarm clock, but by my barking buddy, Bloopers.

"Bloopers, why are you making so much noise?" I yelled. I fed him and rushed him out to poop. After a messy poop clean up, we went back in. On my way to school feeling a little tired from yesterday's events, I thought about how I was maturing and thinking smarter than usual.

"Hello Johnson," greeted Mrs. Hill.

"Hello and good morning ma'am," I replied.

WHAT ABOUT JOHNSON?

"Hello class! Today we will talk about numbers and how they operate."

After math class I saw Gee and one of the boys that played basketball with us walking down the hall. As we greeted one another, I noticed the boy with Gee had on a neck brace. I never did ask him his name, but I wondered what happened knowing the brace wasn't there a week or so ago, so I inquired about it. He told me he was in a car accident and one of his friends that were in the car with them is in the hospital. Feeling bad about it, I gave my condolences to him and the boy's family. "So Gee, what homeroom are you in?" I asked.

"I'm in Mr. Wilson's class, he's cool."

"Oh ok. I'll talk to you guys later. I have to get to class now."

I spotted Michael on the way to class. "Yo Michael!" I yelled down the hall. "What's going on?"

"What's going on Johnson?"

"A whole lot Michael. I have some things I need to talk to you about and need to meet with you."

"Okay, we can meet by the front door after school."

"Cool."

After the school bell sounded off, I rushed to get my things without looking back. After waiting about five minutes, I felt someone tap me on my shoulder. It was Michael.

"Come on man let's get out of here," he suggested.

"Hey Michael, you won't believe what Lisa said to me the other day." At first, I didn't tell him because I wanted him to guess what it was.

"Come on man, tell me what she said. Spill the beans man," he begged.

"Okay, okay, she told me she always liked me." I was smiling from ear to ear.

"Yeah right."

"No really, she told me two days ago and I was as shocked as you are now."

"Man, Lisa is one of the prettiest girls in school! And she likes my best friend? So what are you going to do?"

"You know we are too young to have girlfriends, so what can I do?"

"Does she know you have the hots for her too?" Michael asked.

"Yes."

"Okay, so at least now you know and can now be friends with a crush."

"Great advice. See Michael that's why I like you, because you think somewhat like me and always give good feedback."

"We're friends to the end like Chucky!" Michael joked.

"Yeah, like Chucky," I laughed.

"Hey Mike, my mom's friend Frank brought me a puppy and I named him Bloopers."

"Bloopers? What kind of name is that?"

"I like that name man, so don't make fun of my guard dog."

"Guard dog? He sounds more like a circus clown."

I punched Michael on the arm as we both laughed. "Well Johnson, that's your dog and as long as you and Bloopers are happy that's all that counts, but Bloopers is still a funny name!"

"Ok Michael, I'm turning here. I'll catch up with you later. Maybe you can stop by later and see the dog you made fun of."

"Sure," Michael agreed.

CHAPTER TEN

On the way home I saw the same homeless man I had given the three dollars and Now and Laters to. As I approached him, he looked at me as though he recognized me.

"Excuse me young man, can I ask you a question?" I was kind of surprised because not only a stranger, but a homeless man wanted to talk to me.

"Sure you can."

"Are you the kid that gave me the three dollars and the Now and Laters about a month ago?"

"Yes sir, that was me."

He stated that sometimes people do give him money and sometimes food, but never has he been given anything by a kid. "I really appreciate what you did. God will bless you for it." He also said I should stay in school to get a good education. "Always, always, listen to your parents."

He told me he used to go to school a long time ago but dropped out in the seventh grade. The man told me if he could take it all back he would because there is no life being homeless; it's unhealthy and it is sad.

As I was about to leave the homeless man said, "It's too late for me to get back on track, so all I can do now is pray and try to help others along the way. I will work for food and money, but most people won't hire me because of my condition. Oh, and my name is Tom," he said, extending his hand. "Feel free to talk to me anytime."

"Thanks Tom, it was a pleasure meeting you sir and I will take your advice," I replied, shaking his hand. "Be blessed." I told him things will get better and I will pray for him to get off the streets. I started to walk away, only to be called back by Tom.

"What's this?" I asked puzzled, as Tom gave me the shiny 1716 gold coin.

"Well son, I was holding on to this coin for some time now and something told me to give it to you." After accepting the odd but rare looking coin, I said thank you very much and walked away, leaving Tom in tears.

"Mom, mom! Look what Tom gave me."

"What is it baby?" mom asked, looking closely at the shiny gold coin. "Who gave this to you?"

"Tom. He's the homeless man I gave the candy and money to about a month ago. I don't know why, but when I was walking away he gave it to me and said he wanted me to have it."

"This is a very old quarter baby and it's worth a lot of money, probably thousands. Let me hold on to it and we will figure out what to do with it later. Ok?"

"Yes mom." I had no clue as to what was in my possession, but would later be very happy about it's worth.

"Mom can I go out to the park and take Bloopers with me?"

"Did you do your homework?"

"Yes, I did it in school."

"Ok, that's fine. Don't let anything happen to that dog."

This would be my first long adventure with my furry friend. I started to walk with Bloopers and heard a crashing sound behind me. I looked to see what it was and noticed the three car accident. There was glass and pieces of broken metal all over the place. I prayed everyone was ok as I crossed Rockaway Parkway and Saint John Street. As I got closer to the entrance of the park, I noticed the multitude of people there. I looked over towards the basketball courts and saw Gee and the other two boys that were with him a few days ago.

"Johnson what's going on man, is that your dog?" Gee asked.

"Yes it is. This is Bloopers."

"I'm sorry again for what happened to your face from the basketball game the other day."

"It's ok. I'm fine."

"Looks like we won't be playing basketball today because no one has a ball and you have your guard dog with you," said Gee.

Next thing you know six boys walked over to us and asked us where we were from. The boys were a little bigger and taller than we were. After they all said their names, I stood silenced, saying nothing at all.

"What about you?" one of the boys asked, looking at me. As I stood still not saying a word, one of the boys reached over to pick up Bloopers. I quickly picked up the dog to shelter him under my arm.

"What are you doing?" I asked the boy. Greg and his friends looked on as though they would help or protect

What About Johnson?

me if need be, because I was now considered to be their friend.

Greg quickly stepped in telling them to leave us alone or he will get his big brother on them. As the kids moved closer, one of them asked Gee who his big brother was. Gee responded with, "Big Bee."

Although no one, not even Greg's friends, knew who Big Bee was, no one wanted to find out or take the chance. As the six troublemakers left, Gee, the others, and I started laughing out loud.

"They're fools, they only picked on us because we're smaller than they are, but when I mentioned my big bad brother Bee they ran away." Gee said.

We all left the park to go home, that was enough drama for the day. "Ok guys, I'll see ya'll later."

"Ok, Johnson." They all said.

"His big bad brother Bee," I laughed. Gee used psychology on them and it worked. "Wait until I tell mommy about this," I said to Bloopers. "Come on Bloopers, let's go home and get something to eat. It's getting cold out."

"Is everything ok baby?" mom asked.

77

"Yes mom, but these older boys were starting trouble with my friends and me at the park."

After telling my mother what happened she told me to be careful. My mother knew she couldn't be with me everywhere I went, but told me if I was ever in trouble to come straight home.

It was December and less than a week before Christmas. Although it didn't feel that cold, riding a bike with the wind chill would make it colder. I never thought much about Christmas and all the gift exchanging, but I always got the gift I wanted. This year I told my mom that wanted an iPod or a cell phone.

I thought; why not call Junior to see if he wants to come over to spend the night. School was out for a whole week because of Christmas, we could catch up on things and I could help him study.

Mom knew I had been showing responsible and positive signs lately, so she said, "Of course you can, here's fifty cents to call him and come right back. After calling Junior and speaking to Aunty Ann, she agreed to let Junior come over. After she told me he was packing his books and things, I hung up.

"Mom, Aunty Ann said its fine with her and he's on his way."

After opening the door for Junior we both ran up to my room as Junior yelled out, "Hello Aunty Renay."

"Listen Junior, Lisa likes me, this is my dog Bloopers, and Tom gave me a very old quarter."

"Calm down," he said. "We got all day to talk."

"I know, I know. But let me tell you what Lisa said a few days ago." Although we were up late, we continued to talk until we were tired. We both fell asleep in the middle of our conversation. As I slept, I dreamed about homeless men. I had this dream before, but this dream was a little different. This time they were laughing and chanting,

"Johnson! Johnson!"

I thought I saw Tom in my dream but couldn't recognize him because it was cold and the man had on a wool hat with a scarf wrapped tightly around his face. As I was about to walk over to the man in my dream, to see if it was Tom or not, I heard a dog barking loudly. I realized it was Bloopers.

"Junior, I just had the craziest dream," I said, as Junior turned back over, falling back to sleep. I wondered if this dream had any meaning at all. "Lie down and go back to sleep dog. Shut up Bloopers." I was tired and just wanted to get back to sleep.

When I woke up, Junior was still sleep. I walked Bloopers and fed him. When I came back into the house, I let Bloopers sniff and lick Junior's face. Junior really did have a big balloon shaped head. I made funny faces at him while he was asleep until he opened his eyes and caught me. He looked at me as if he had forgotten he stayed the night over. He jumped up and chased me around until my mom told us to stop making so much noise in the morning. I helped Junior with his school work and studied with him for about an hour and a half before we ate breakfast. Junior and I walked to the library to get a book called 'People Helping People'. We couldn't find the book, but I was determined to find a book Junior could read to help him respect and know more about responsibilities.

"Let's go in the family section to get a book on family matters." I suggested.

We weren't going to leave that library until we found a book that dealt with love, respect and family. "Got it!" I said. "Here take this one." 'Family Matters' was the name of the book I picked up.

"Come on Junior, let's get out of here, I got some writing to do and you have to go home soon."

I decided to have Junior help me clean my room before he left to go home. Sometimes my mother and I would talk at the kitchen table, but she was busy at the moment. I sat at the table and thought about how nice it would be if everyone in the world would take the time to talk to one another. I thought about how only seven months ago I wasn't much of a talker, and in fact quite antisocial. I came a long way for a kid my age with only one parent. Thinking of the pain many other kids my age go through now affected me, knowing I too was there not long ago. I knew the first step to receive help is to be receptive to suggestions.

CHAPTER ELEVEN

As I looked out my window I saw people walking, teenagers smoking cigarettes, and noticed three guy's making some kind of deal. As my mind started to run away, snow flurries caught my eye. *Nice!*

I liked snow and couldn't wait until it stuck so I could make a snow man and use a carrot for the nose. As I sat mesmerized by the amount of snow that sat on my window sill, a man I've never seen before pushed our door bell and was looking up at our window.

"Mom! Some man is at the door." Mom knew who it was at the door and told me to open it. After I opened the door, the man I would soon call dad was walking behind me as I walked up the stairs.

"How are you?" he asked.

"I'm fine sir," I answered.

He called me son, but I didn't pay it much attention because most men call boys son.

"Baby," my mother said, "this is your father and his name is James. James Johnson."

It felt so strange knowing soon I would be calling this man dad. My father was about five feet, ten inches tall with a medium build. He had a nice smile and a warm heart.

"Come and give your dad a hug."

So many questions were running through my mind, but the first one I wanted to ask was where have you been all this time and why now? I knew it was a sensitive issue to discuss at the present time, so I waited. When I hugged him he smelled like old spice and a used cigar.

He finally said, "I know you have many questions and I will answer all of them in due time."

He told me I have a step-brother by the name of Greg, and that Greg and I are the same age. "If it's ok with your mother you can come over for a few days now that school will be out for a week or so."

I thought this timing couldn't be better. Christmas is only days away, I met my father for the first time, and will meet my step-brother Greg.

"Mom, can I go please?"

Waht About Johnson?

My mother looked at me as if she were surprised I was so quick to go with this man I barely knew, but this was my dad.

"Sure baby, go pack a bag for two days and don't forget your toothbrush."

"Thanks mom."

"We have a very respectful boy," my dad said to my mother. He went on to explain how sorry he was for not being a part of my life, but will be there from now on to help with anything he can.

My father had a nice car. I think it was a BMW. After driving about five minutes and listening to jazz music, we finally arrived. The building was a brown stone with all marble floors throughout the building. As my father and I took the elevator to his third floor apartment, I looked at my father and said, "Thanks dad." I could tell my father was startled.

"You're welcome, but why are you thanking me?"

"Just because," I replied, as the door swung open.

"Gee?" I couldn't believe he was standing in front of me!

"Johnson?" said Gee, looking just as confused as me.

We both were shocked.

"You're my brother?" I asked.

"You two have met?" Our dad said.

"Yes dad, this is the boy I was telling you and mom about the other day," Gee explained. "So all this time we were brothers and never knew it."

My father then introduced me to my step-mother. She was a very nice lady. My step-mother was tall with long hair down her back. The first thing she did was give me some warm milk and brownies. I was overwhelmed at the fact I now have family only five minutes away. See, Gee and I never took the time to talk about our family's background and Gee never asked me my first name. We would never have known about each other, but my mother contacted one of her friends and through them was able to contact James. Now that my brother and I have united, we wasted no time catching up on things.

Thinking about how some people manipulate others into doing things is ridiculous. I find it much easier to ask for what you want to know than to trick people and lie. The point I'm making is that at my age, I see and now analyze as some adults do. Some adults don't think us kids can relate to life's matters. When you're faced with issues and forced to deal with things, you do just that. As a child I looked at situations as they were and never turned away. Most kids have no clue that unless they face things head on as facts, they too will fail and fall to deceit, manipulation, and possibly have insecurity issues. My mother only knew what I wanted to tell her, and although she could sometimes see through the mental mask I wore, it was important for me to completely open up to get the proper love and help I needed as a child.

I can't imagine living without my mother, but the reality of it is that one day she too will die. My father told me he always thought about me, but wasn't ready for a child. He told me when he met his wife she already had a son and that Greg was only seven when they met. My father told me he always talked about me to his wife and friends, and that his love for me will never change. That day my mother told my father that I wanted an iPod or a cell phone for Christmas. If I had not known, I would have thought this was all just a dream, and that a message of love, hope, and wisdom was to be imbedded into my memory banks. It's never easy to trust, but we must learn to use our instincts and hearts to understand people at times.

My brother Gee was somewhat like myself, and although we were about the same height, age, and complexion, I knew we were only step brothers. We left to go to my father's favorite Italian restaurant to eat. After a very good dinner we all went home. It was getting late so Greg and I played with his baseball cards and talked.

After two days I was ready to go home to mom. I missed her and wanted to see her. As soon as I reached the top of the stairs I gave my father a hug and told my brother I would be seeing him in school and on the basketball court to learn some of his moves. As they walked off the porch and across the street, I watched from our front window.

"You'll be seeing a lot of them," mom said. She could see the bond I formed with my father in a matter of days. She said that one day I will go to live with my dad and step brother. Thoughts of not living with my mother were unheard of, but I was ready for the change and had so much catching up to do. By now my grades had gone up and Lisa and I no longer studied. I really do thank Lisa because she has helped me tremendously. I would love to get her a gift for Christmas for helping me.

What would she like? I said to myself. *I'll just spend about ten dollars and look for something colorful.* I thought that if I was going to buy my mother something what would it be and what can she use? *Ok, why not just buy Lisa a matching scarf and hat set? Perfect! She would like that.* My mother walked into my room and asked me if I was ok.

"Yes mom."

After asking her about the coin Tom had given me, she said tomorrow we would go to get the coin appraised. That night while playing with Bloopers, I had plans for the money I was going to get from the 1716 gold coin. With no school and tomorrow being Christmas, I went to sleep. The faster I go to sleep the sooner I can get up to get my Christmas gifts, although we didn't have a Christmas tree put up.

Christmas morning arrived and even though there was no tree, decorations, or presents, I knew mom had something up her sleeve. I wasn't yet an adult so of course I was expecting a gift of some sort. Besides, even if my mother couldn't get me a gift because of her income, my instincts told me today was going to be good.

CHAPTER TWELVE

My mother told me to get dressed so we could go to the coin collector. She told me to dress warm because there's a foot of snow outside. We walked in the foot high snow even as snow continued to fall. With only two more blocks before we reached the train, I told my mother what I wanted to do with some of the money if the coin was worth more than expected. She told me that was nice, but she hopes it is also because she could use it to put me in college.

We walked inside the tall sky scraper onto an elevator and exited on the thirty-first floor. A slim lady at the receptionist desk asked if she could help us. My mother asked to speak to John and let the receptionist know he was expecting us. She pointed us to the left as we looked towards that direction.

"Yes. Ms. Johnson I presume?" John said.

"Yes sir."

"Have a seat please. So you have a coin you want me to take a look at, correct?"

"Yes, that's correct."

The moment my mother handed John the rare and shiny coin, he didn't take his eyes off the coin, not even to look back towards our direction. He looked at the coin carefully with a magnifying glass.

"Very interesting, where did you get this coin?" John asked my mother.

"Some homeless man by the name of Tom gave it to my son."

"Hmmm, Well Ms. Johnson, you and your son have an incredibly valuable coin estimated at about sixty-seven thousand dollars."

"Did you say sixty-seven thousand dollars Mr. John?"

"That's correct ma'am. This coin is exceptionally rare and is in excellent condition and should be placed in a vault for protection."

He said he would write a check for the sixty seven thousand dollars now if she was willing to sell it. My mother looked at me as if she was waiting for my approval on the deal. Not that she needed my approval, she's my mother. I love and trust all of her decisions. I was only ten, but I knew the value of sixty-seven thousand dollars.

"I'll take it," mom said.

After we made the transaction and signed some papers, John handed my mom the check and told her he could cash it there for her if she wanted. We both were overwhelmed and speechless when we took the cash. When John gave my mother the cash she said, "Thank you sir, such a pleasure doing business with you."

The first thing I wanted to do with the money was to buy my mother something nice and expensive. "Mom, can I please have a hundred dollars."

"Sure baby, but what do you want a hundred dollars for?"

"I wanted to buy you and Lisa something while we were here in Manhattan with the money."

When we walked into Macy's I immediately saw the gold chain I wanted my mother to have. The chain was small, but had a heart on it and cost seventy-nine dollars. After I brought the chain and a nice scarf and glove set, we left to go home with all our cash. When we arrived home my dad, brother, and step mother were parked outside and greeted us. They looked so happy as they all handed me a gift individually.

There were two gifts, plus a Christmas card. I hugged and kissed my brother on the cheek. The bond that my brother and I built from the start was genuine and grew stronger as we realized we were much alike in many ways. I never mentioned the money to my father, but he later found out through my mom.

As they left, I waived at my brother and he waived back. My mother sat me down at the kitchen table and said to me, "Son this is your money and we will do something nice for you with it. What's the biggest thing you want to do with it?"

I told her after I give some to the church I wanted to do something special for the homeless shelter.

"Mommy, I would like to buy food and clothing to give to a homeless shelter."

I suddenly thought of Tom. "If it wasn't for Tom none of this would be possible."

I knew one day I would see Tom and give him money to find a place for him to stay.

"Oh my gosh, I forgot to get my brother something for Christmas!"

It wasn't until then that I realized that Gee and I had received the best Christmas gift ever, our relationship. When I walked into my room Bloopers was so happy to see me. I couldn't walk to my bed without dodging him.

"Okay Bloopers, I know you love me, now let me put my things down please."

My mother and I had a nice Christmas after all. We talked about putting me in college after I finished high school. Now that we had this money, I remembered what Tom said about furthering my education, so college was definitely a possibility. There was a certain level of peace I had once I settled in and thought about what took place two hours ago. I walked into my room and noticed dog doo on the floor.

"Oh no, we've got to get you trained real soon." I picked Bloopers up to put his face close to the dog doo and smacked him on the butt to let him know there was no pooping in the house. As I was walking past my mother's bedroom door with dog doo, I peeked in her door and said, "Hi mom, I love you."

"I love you too! We'll go food shopping tomorrow to pick up some things and we will also go clothes shopping, alright?"

I couldn't wait to give Lisa her Christmas gift. Speaking of Christmas gifts, I almost forgot to open the gifts on my bed. Although both boxes were small I decided to open the bigger box first.

"Oh my gosh! A cell phone!" I always wanted a cell phone and it was the exact one I wanted; a BlackBerry touch screen. Could the other box be an iPod? I tore the Christmas wrap off the box.

"Yes! My iPod! Mommy look!"

"That's nice baby."

I knew my mother told my father what I wanted for Christmas.

"Isn't that what you wanted baby?" she asked.

"Yes, and it's the right color too."

By now I was exhausted and wanted to relax and rest. Two minutes after I laid down my mother opened my door so I could hear my favorite Christmas song, Rudolph the Red Nosed Reindeer. That song touched me deeply for some reason but I couldn't figure out why. It wasn't like I never heard the song before. Maybe it was because I was still excited about the money, it being Christmas, and all my emotions were running high. As tears started to flow down my cheek I thought about my very first Christmas gift. It was a Play Station system with two games I wanted. Just when I thought things were getting worse, it got better. Because of the money, mommy and I lived a lot easier and didn't struggle as much.

Christmas was over. Now it is time to get back to business as usual. I knew returning back to school would be fun, especially now that I had new clothes, a bike, Bloopers, and my Christmas gifts. I knew that no matter what happened from here on, I would change for the better. I was always told that money is the root of all evil and to stay true to yourself at all times, even if success knocks at your door. I didn't know if I would see Lisa at school tomorrow, but packed her Christmas gifts in my backpack just in case.

My alarm clock was ringing.

"Baby get up!" my mom yelled out.

"My batteries must be low mom, because I didn't hear the alarm. It sounds weak."

After freshening up and walking Bloopers, I now looked at life differently. Many things had happened, and my ability to process information and to correct mistakes had increased. My mother told me not to mention anything about the money to anyone. She also told me there are bad people out there who will try to manipulate, lie, and steal to get the large amount of money we had.

"Okay mom, I won't."

I began walking to school feeling confident and smarter. I was focused on being a better person. My thoughts were interrupted by Michael.

"Johnson, you look sharp!"

"Thanks Michael."

"So Johnson, how was your Christmas? Did you get a lot of gifts?

"Yes! It was very special and I was tremendously blessed."

"What does blessed mean?" asked Michael.

"It means when God does something special for you. Michael, remember the boy at the park named Gee I told you about? Well, he's my brother!"

"Say what?"

"That's right, he's my brother."

"When did you find that out?"

"Just a few days ago. There is so much more I want to tell you, but was told not to by my mother."

The closer we got to the school the more you could tell a holiday had just passed because of the new clothes most of the kids had on and the gadgets the kids sported.

"Hello Gee," I said, as he walked towards me and Michael.

"What's up brother?" he responded.

"Michael, this is my brother Gee I told you about."

"Hello Gee," Michael spoke.

"Hey Michael, did you see Lisa around?" I asked.

"No not yet."

"Okay brother, I will see you later. I have to get to class," Gee announced, walking fast in the opposite direction.

Mrs. Hill wasn't in class today, but we did have a young substitute teacher that had no patience at all.

"Ok class, hurry up and take out your notes that Mrs. Hill gave you to study," the teacher ordered. *This was going to be a long day.*

When school let out I rushed to leave, hoping I might run into Lisa. Just when I was turning the corner I saw Lisa's friend, Kathy.

"Kathy, have you seen Lisa today?"

"Yes. She's walking with a couple of girls about a block away."

After running a block down, I spotted Lisa. She looked really nice wearing a red sweat suit with black Reeboks. Her hair was in cornrolls and she sported a black, bubble down, waist length goose down coat.

"Hey Lisa."

"Hi Johnson, on your way home I see."

"Yeah. Hey listen, I brought you a little something for Christmas."

"Thank you Johnson."

"This is very pretty and I see you have good taste too."

"You're welcome Lisa."

"I'm sorry I wasn't able to get you anything."

"That's okay; I got everything I wanted for Christmas and more."

"Did you pass your test you were studying so hard for?" she asked.

"Yes, I scored a ninety- three on it."

"That's great."

"Ok." I said. "I will talk to you later."

"Ok, bye Johnson."

Lisa knows I like her and every time she wears her scarf and hat set she will think about me.

CHAPTER THIRTEEN

Taking the short cut home from school, I deviated to see if I would see someone who I now considered a friend, Tom. The weather was dreadfully cold and I knew Tom didn't have anything to wear except the clothes on his back. I hoped to see him so I could invite him over to my home to discuss how we were going to get him food and off the streets.

I walked by the corner store that he once called home. That's when I saw a bunch of candles and flowers near where he always laid. I've seen this site before; you know the candles, flowers, teddy bears etc., but I never understood or inquired about it. I was curious as to why things were placed in that very same area and I questioned the store owner.

The store owner told me a man by the name of Tom Becker died there yesterday and the flowers are from people leaving their condolences. I asked him if the man was homeless and he shook his head yes. He said Tom must have died due to the cold weather and that he had made the front page in the New York Post.

I was angry after hearing that. I bought two packs of Now and Laters and sat them next to the candles with three, one dollar bills. I ran the rest of the way home in tears, feeling a slight asthma attack coming on due to the cold. I began to panic. While searching for my asthma pump, my breathing became difficult and chest pains began to occur. I broke the key trying to get in the door. All I could do was pray that mom was home to doctor me back to normal. Bang! Bang! I pounded on the door and my mother quickly opened it.

"What's the matter baby?" She knew at once what the problem was because she'd seen it many times before. "Sit here," she ordered.

"Mom--" I started.

"Don't talk, use the pump I told you to keep with you at all times."

"Mommy, Tom is dead!" I gasped, still struggling to breathe.

"Who?"

"Tom, mom! He's dead."

"How do you know that son?"

"The man at the store where Tom used to sleep told me on the way home."

"Really?"

"Mom, remember when I told you I wanted to do something special for the homeless? Well I want to donate money to a shelter, but I'm not sure how much."

"How much do you think is good to give son?"

"Since we have a lot of money that was practically given to us, so how about five thousand dollars?"

"Boy, that is a lot of money, but if that's what's in your heart then that's what we will give."

"Thanks mom."

"No problem baby. I know of a shelter that's four blocks down the street that we can give the money to. We will go there tomorrow after you come home from school. Tom would have liked that."

I wasn't feeling well and stayed in the house all day. All I did was play with my Play Station games and rest. The day went by really fast and my mother was right there beside me checking on me every so often. So many things started running through my mind. I started to think about this, that, Tom, and all the trials and situations I was going through. Not many homeless people have friends and Tom probably didn't have many friends or family.

I was falling fast asleep as Bloopers licked my face, as if he knew I was wounded goods. Feeling my blanket slightly being pulled over my shoulder and a soft kiss on my cheek, I slept like a baby.

The next morning my mother brought my new cell phone that I got for Christmas to me. She had gotten one for herself and already stored her number in it in case of emergency or if I needed to call her. I was told not to use it in school and to never let anyone else use it. She told me how to dial 9-1-1 and even gotten a case to keep it in. Now that I had a cell phone I couldn't wait to use it. Sometimes I would see other kids with cell phones, iPods and other gadgets and wouldn't be jealous, but had always wished I had one also. I wanted my best friend Michael and my cousin Junior to have one, but with everything else in life comes responsibility.

After passing by my bike in the hallway, thoughts of riding next year with my brother and Michael occurred. I would love for Junior to ride with us, but he lives too far to ride his bike to my house. Anyway, next year would be a good one and I had plans of buying Michael a used bike, if not a new one because that's what friends are for.

"Good Morning." Mrs. Hill greeted the class. "Did my boys and girls have a good Christmas and happy new year?"

It was good to see our teacher back and like last year, she brought everyone cookies and candy, which I couldn't wait to eat. In the cafeteria, Michael and I talked about graduation and where we wanted our parents to take us. We also talked about his parents moving to another state which meant I wouldn't see him anymore. I had lost Tom and may now lose my best friend of three years. Michael also got a cell phone for Christmas so we exchanged numbers. At least now we could call each other to talk about things. We walked out of school together laughing at some boy who had his pants really low, showing the crack of his butt.

"Michael why do boys wear their pants that low and how could they run if they were being chased by a mean pit?"

Michael laughed at the thought and said, "I don't know, but he needs to change his underwear." We both laughed so hard. Michael and I were very close and our friendship became unbreakable. Now that Michael, Greg, and I communicated, the three of us together were a hilarious sight to imagine. Hearing the sound of a cell phone ringing in my pocket startled me. It was my mother calling me to hurry home so we could go to the shelter to donate the money.

"Ok mom, I'm on my way."

After the call was disconnected, I felt kind of responsible. I felt like others were somehow depending on me, and in no way would I let them down. I wanted to be responsible and independent. I also wanted people to like me.

"Michael I will call you later," I yelled out before turning the corner of my block.

"See you later Johnson!"

I called my mother and told her to come down stairs a half a block away.

"Boy, you are growing up so fast and mommy is so proud of you. Your grandmother told me you were going to make it in life and make some special lady very happy."

I smiled. "I've already started mom!"

Mom looked at me and smiled as her cell phone rang. "Hello? Yes this is Mrs. Johnson, I'm about a block away. Ok. See you shortly."

"Was that the shelter's director calling you mom?"

"Yes it was baby."

As we entered the shelter, I noticed the many signs that were hanging over most of the walls.

"Hello Mrs. Johnson, we were expecting you and we appreciate your enormous financial donation to our men's shelter. My name is Barbara and our director David will be with you shortly. "

"Thank you."

As my mother and I waited, we saw men leaving and entering the building. Some of the men looked like they could use a hygiene confrontation from the director himself. Many of the men coming in had garbage bags filled with their personal belongings. It really did hurt my mother and me, but the reality of it is not everyone out there wants help.

A very tall man introduced himself as David and welcomed us with open arms. As my mother handed him the five thousand dollars in cash, he said, "This money will help the men with shelter, food and clothing. Most of the homeless go out to look for work after receiving health care and the proper identification to seek employment. Not too many people donate money in large amounts, but we believe that God blesses people who bless others."

He turned to me. "You are a wise young man and your mother told me it was your idea to donate this money. We need more kids like you in this world. Thank you young man, we will send you a letter of appreciation in the mail." He gave me some candy as we stood up to leave.

"Thank you, we must go now," I said, grabbing my mother's hand.

We left to go to my favorite restaurant, Mickey Dee's. My mother always talked about getting her driver's license. We could afford a car now, but decided to wait until the time was right. I was expecting to have my driver's license at age seventeen. I believed men should have their license because it is a big part of being independent. I wanted to be like those men that handled business properly. I figure since I have started to mature, why not go all the way? *Could I be setting myself up for major disappointment, due to me maturing at a fast pace?*

Following through was my New Year's resolution which many people failed due to lack of dedication. On the way home, mom and I stopped at the pet store to get a dog cage for barking Bloopers. Bloopers has now learned to stay, and sit. Spending quality time with Bloopers has made it easier for him to learn, I believe that animals show love to those who love them.

CHAPTER FOURTEEN

Thinking how much my mother has done for me my entire life made me want to do something super special to show my appreciation. Though mom had control of the money, it belonged to me, so she wouldn't have a problem if I told her to treat herself to something expensive from me. She did. Three stores down from the pet store was a jewelry store. She brought a diamond necklace and a diamond bracelet with matching earrings. She looked like a million bucks, and her smile warmed my heart. I knew I was the man in her life that made her the happiest woman on earth. My mother and I now had the best mother and son relationship ever. It was because we confided in each other on things that some parents wouldn't dare touch. It wasn't until then that I knew I could confide in her about anything, everything, and anyone. I mean, if no one else, we should always be able to talk to and trust our parents. My mother did later experience some things which I care not to talk about, but we all will and do have our own battles and problems to face. She's been clean for quite some time and lives life one day at a time. She's the best mom, and I wouldn't trade her in for anything or anyone!

My friend Michael also matured as life went on. Michael continually showed me what a true friend was all about and never at any point had envy or jealousy, but always love and respect. At our age, it's much easier to have friends and not worry about too many things because being ten isn't that hard, but there are challenges that may arrive. Michael will do well, and I will be there for him as much as possible. He is sarcastic at times, but that's what makes him Michael.

Big headed Junior has improved in all school work. He's getting A's and B's and many of the kids that were a bad influence in his life no longer exist. He started taking karate classes which taught respect, discipline, and self defense. Junior's overall attitude and behavior have trickled down to at least two of his friends who also now lead by example. He's now what some may consider a role model kid.

Now Lisa, sad to say, I heard she was moving down south after graduation. I know that one day we will see each other again because she's a true friend indeed. She was always smart and would always finish what she started. She's very talented for someone her age and I never knew she could sing the way she does. Her parents opened up a grocery store down south where she works as a cashier part-time. Plus, I have a picture of her she gave me in the lunch room cafeteria that I forgot to give back to her. She'll always be someone special to me and be remembered as little Lisa.

I was smiling and feeling the joy as Gee, the first kid that nearly gave me my first black eye from a basketball, called me on my cell phone. I'm glad to have a brother to grow and mature with me, as I try to learn his amazing Michael Jordan moves. Gee is also a B+ student and made honor roll three times in a row. It's almost as if we were meant to be biological brothers because we look alike, except I'm more handsome than he is. Ha! Ha! My brother Gee is always smiling, and that's one of his characteristics I'd like to adopt. We're like a magnet on iron and continue to get stronger together.

Aunty MaryAnn had a beautiful baby girl which she named Destiny. She opened up a day care center three months ago after the birth of her daughter. The timing was perfect for her because with Junior on track, baby born, and business running smooth, life didn't seem so bad after all. She also hired my mother at her day care center for full time employment. I myself started reading part two of 'What *About Johnson?*' because I really liked the first one. Part one was only the second book I've ever read and I knew part two would be even better. Someone once told me that I should at least read ten books a year to keep my mind sharp, so I'm attempting to be consistent with that.

Accepting the conditions in this world that need to be changed is what I'm up against. Although my view points at my age are to be taken into consideration, many may overlook them due to their lack of understanding maturity. The knowledge that I seek, I wish to influence other minors so that they too may one day lead other kids, even adults, to vision and understand their mentality. Even my mom may have been at one point misled by mixed emotions, believing she understood what I believed.

My mother listens and pays more attention to me now more than ever because my communication, motives, and attention span have increased considerably. I'm thinking of writing my own book one day. I don't know what I would call it or if it would ever be published, but I was told that reading and writing is part of expanding my mind.

My father is in my life now and we have a bond as though he was always there. I also started taking karate classes for the purpose of discipline and self defense. My mother thought it would be a good idea because I may need to defend myself one day. Because of Tom, I can now look forward to going to college. Every time I walk past the corner store I think of Tom and wished he had a second chance at life. The candles are still there, but nothing else is. Even though I located the article the day he died, it wouldn't bring him back, but it made me feel better and gave me closure. Tom will be missed.

There are many good parents out there who try their hardest to raise their children the best they can. I know for sure that kids sometimes manipulate their parents to get what they want. Parents know, they were kids once and obviously at some point used manipulation tactics daily. I felt as though the more I learned, the more I could teach as long as my advice and information is accurate. Not only am I no longer quiet and shy, I have more friends and I am no longer isolated. I'm also persistent in completing and following through with most things. I'm so glad I no longer feel like I'm wearing a mask and people now understand me. There were times when I looked or talked to people, even my mother at times, and felt as if they were looking straight through me during our conversation. My teacher, Mrs. Hill, always encouraged me to do good, knowing my intentions were beneficial to others around me.

That summer, my first business attempt was to open up a lemonade stand which turned out to be very successful, due to my ability to communicate with others. As a child, I never got a spanking from my parents. I always did as I was told even if I didn't want to. I tell my friends that their parents aren't going to tell them to do something wrong, but if they do, kids need to seek advice from another adult such as the other parent, an aunt, or even a sibling. Like my mother told me once, we all have instincts and should use them to better our judgment. I used to believe most things I was told, but destined now to investigate and research before believing. It's been pretty encouraging and quite interesting. Even now, I must remember that I'm only ten and have my whole life ahead of me.

The End

Look for *'What About Johnson? Two'* coming to stores near you real soon.

"Believe it."

At seven-thirty in the morning, I lifted the gates to the candy store I worked at since the age of thirteen. Unlocking the door as I picked up the New York Post the paper boy left, I entered the store. *What a beautiful morning, I* thought as I sipped on my Bustelo coffee.

About the Author

Harvell Johnson III is forty-four years old and has two sons that he loves dearly. Harvell Johnson grew up in New York and lived alone with his mother in Bedford Stuyvesant, Brooklyn until age twelve. He always wanted to write a book about and for kids; a book that even adults could read to find knowledgeable and useful information on raising and building a trustful relationship with their kids.

He's an amazing song writer, inventor, and entrepreneur who believes in focusing on what's most important to get the best results in life. He's a Christian man who challenged life head on and won the battle of transition and now lives each day as if it were his last. Now living in Allentown, Pennsylvania, he continues to write and invent along with his other talents and skills.

Harvell's goal is to help as many people as possible to make the world a better place for all.

For comments or feedback, e-mail Harvell Johnson at:
hjchristian22@gmail.com or write to him at:
Harvell Johnson
PO Box 4294
Allentown, PA 18105

Friend on Facebook
www.facebook.com/harvell.johnson

Made in the USA
Middletown, DE
20 April 2021

37389949R00075